The Night Terrors

Written & Illustrated By
Pete Woolgar

DEDICATIONS & THANKS

For Sophie & Ted.

Dedicated to any children (and grown-ups) who are scared of the dark.

Thanks to RePrint Brighton for your fabulous support.

Daisy used to hate bedtime.
I know every child hates bedtime, don't they?
But Daisy REALLY hated bedtime!

It wasn't just because she wanted to stay up late... it was because of the dark, and the things that kept happening in the dark.

It seemed like almost every night
that poor little Daisy suffered a fright.

Some nights she heard banging and twanging.

Other nights she would see mysterious shadows in her room.

And she had even heard "Wooooing" type noises coming from somewhere!

It seemed like almost every night
that poor little Daisy suffered a fright.

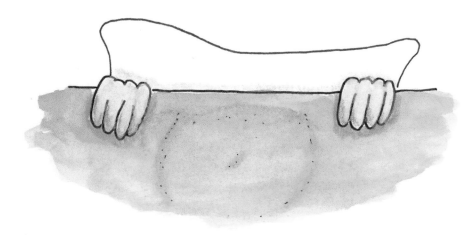

Daisy was scared of the monsters, creatures and ghosts that she was sure came out at night.

No matter how many times the grown-ups told her not to worry and that monsters didn't exist, Daisy just couldn't get over her fear.

One night, everything changed.

Daisy was half dreaming, and half awake when she suddenly heard a thudding, thumping noise.

She was now wide awake, and her heart was racing!

Then she heard a screech from the wardrobe.

It was awful!

Daisy was so scared that she couldn't even scream.

Did she really have a creature in her wardrobe?!

And now there was a noise coming from under her bed.

Was there a monster under her bed too?!

Everything that Daisy had feared was happening all at once, and it was terrifying! And then, to top it all off, she saw a huge dark shadow moving around her room. It was obviously very dark, but it was definitely there!

It seemed like almost every night
that poor little Daisy suffered a fright,
but this was the worst night of all.

Daisy was so scared, but she knew she had to do something.

She took a couple of deep breaths and used all the courage that she could muster to jump out of bed and switch on the light...

And there they were!

"Who are you!?" Daisy whispered, angrily.
"And what are you doing?!"

"I'm very sorry. I am The Boogie Man and I love to dance whilst my friends play music."

"Oh dear! I am The Guitar Playing Ghost from the wardrobe.
I didn't mean to scare you; I didn't even mean to wake you."

"And I'm The Darkness Drummer, I really didn't mean for you to hear me go bump in the night."

"Yes, and I am sorry for hiding under your bed, I was just warming up my voice before rehearsals.
We're all in a band, and we call ourselves 'The Night Terrors'... you could say that I am 'The Rock Star Under Your Bed'!"

Daisy took a moment to allow what she had just heard to sink in.

"Ok, so you're all in a band?
And all the things I was scared of: things going bump, creatures in my wardrobe, Boogie Men and Rock Stars... I mean *monsters* under my bed, is just you lot?!"

"Yes...sorry."

"This is so...

COOL!"

"So, you're not angry?" asked The Boogie Man.

"And you're not scared?" asked The Guitar Playing Ghost.

"Not anymore!" exclaimed Daisy.
"You all seem really friendly, and I'd love to be in a band, too. Can I join you, please?
I don't play any instruments, but I can sing and dance."

"Absolutely, you can!" said The Rock Star.

"You'll be great in our band!" added The Darkness Drummer.

"Awesome! Thank you."

The band promised to keep the noise down during the week so that they wouldn't disturb Daisy and make her too tired for school.

And Daisy now joins in with the band at weekends and during the school holidays, trying her best not to wake anyone else with the noise.
She has so much fun!

Occasionally Daisy is still woken by bumps in the night or sees shadows or hears strange noises, but she knows it's just the band practising. So, she just smiles, closes her eyes and dreams about the next time she'll be at rehearsals with her monster friends.

Now it's almost every night
that the band perform, to Daisy's delight!

ABOUT THE AUTHOR

Pete Woolgar

Hi there, I'm Pete and I am an illustrator and author.
I have lots of ideas floating around and would love to shape them into more wonderful books in the future.
I have always loved drawing and making up stories since I was a child.

I was always full of energy (getting into mischief) and my mum could only ever keep me quiet by giving me paper
and pencils to occupy my mind! I remember having old rolls of wallpaper to scribble and scrawl on and that
would keep me busy for ages!

I completed an Illustration Diploma with London Art College (in 2017) and it reignited my fire for storytelling.
I had so much fun creating "The Night Terrors" and hope you have enjoyed reading it, too.

You can find me on Instagram and Facebook as "Pete Woolgar Illustrator"
Please keep an eye out for my future projects.
Thank you
Pete

Printed in Great Britain
by Amazon